"Go, Belle!" I whooped with joy.

She picked up speed, but Midnight drew even with her. As soon as she caught sight of him, her neck stretched out and she began to fly over the ground.

She pulled ahead. Midnight dropped back. Then he pulled even again. Belle wasn't having it. Her hooves pounded double time. Midnight fell behind.

We flashed past the spruce tree.

It was over. Already. It seemed to take only seconds to run a quarter mile.

Belle didn't want to stop. As long as Midnight was chasing her, she was going to keep racing. Finally I managed to turn her away after Dad pulled Midnight off in the other direction.

We met back at the spruce tree, both horses panting with happiness.

Andy showed me the stopwatch. "Darn good time you made."

Dad glanced at it and whistled. "Not bad. But more than that, Chris, she showed the instinct. She wasn't going to let Midnight get in front of her."

"You mean—" I grinned so wide a fly could have flown in and out of my mouth and I wouldn't have noticed.

"Yup. You've got a race horse there."

PRIZE-WINNING HORSE, MAYBE

THE DOUBLE DIAMOND DUDE RANCH
#3

By Louise Ladd

AERIE BOOKS LTD.

This is a work of fiction. All the characters and events portrayed in this book are either products of the author's imagination or are used fictitiously.

THE DOUBLE DIAMOND DUDE RANCH #3: PRIZE-WINNING HORSE, MAYBE

Copyright © 1998 by Louise Ladd

Aerie Books Ltd.

First edition: July 1998

Printed in the United States of America

With love to Erika Louise McKeon
and her first pony, Amber.

Acknowledgments

My warmest and deepest thanks to Jim and Bobbi Fetterer, executive directors of the Dude Ranchers' Association. They willingly answered my many questions, offered a number of wonderful ideas, proofread the manuscripts, and generously shared their knowledge of and love for dude ranching.

And a big thank you also to Ellen Hargrave and Tony Bronson at the Hargrave Ranch in Montana, and the Foster family at Lost Valley Ranch in Colorado.

chapter 1

"This foal you're going to have had better turn out to be a prize-winning horse, Belle." I waved the vet's bill under my mare's nose. "Just look at those $ $ $ $ $! He—or she—is sure costing me plenty."

Belle sniffed the paper, then snorted.

"I totally agree." I shoved the bill in my pocket and heaved the saddle onto Belle's back. "It's really your fault, you know. If you hadn't run off last winter and hooked up with that wild mustang—"

"Are you talking to yourself again, Crystal Anne Bradley?" Serena said as she came into the barn.

She was my good friend who lived on the ranch just down the mountain from us and we were the same age, going into sixth grade in the fall.

"No, I'm just holding a discussion with Belle." I

glanced up and noticed Serena was leading Bumper by the halter rope. "Hey, did you bring him in from the pasture yourself?"

"Yup." She looked real proud, and she had a right to. Only a short time ago she was so afraid of horses she couldn't get near them. Now, here she was, walking out in the middle of seventy or so horses and catching the right one.

"Good for you." I felt like giving her three cheers, but there's no sense in overdoing it. "I thought you didn't have time to ride this afternoon."

"Mom and I finished retiling the bathroom earlier than we thought." Serena rolled her dark Chinese-American eyes, to show me how much she did *not* enjoy all the repair work the Changs had to do after they bought the Lazy B. "Then Anna called in a panic, saying the computer ate up the budget figures, so Mom drove up here to the Double Diamond to the rescue and brought me along."

Serena's mom was a computer programmer, and Anna Diamond, who was in charge of all the guests who stayed on our dude ranch, had just bought her first PC to help organize the business.

At least, that was the idea. It seemed like almost every day Anna locked horns with the machine, but that was okay with me. In return for Mrs. Chang's help in sorting out the mess, Serena was free to come riding with me whenever she wanted.

"What were you talking to Belle about?" Serena asked as she fetched her saddle and bridle from the tack room.

"Doctor Cooper's bill came today." I pulled it out of my pocket. "I didn't know how much vets cost. On top of the visits she made to the ranch when Belle got the wrong medicine and scared us all to death, there's the ultrasound exam that told us the foal was okay."

I pulled out another sheet of paper. "Plus, Belle will need more exams before she delivers this winter. Even if nothing else goes wrong, like another accident, just look at what it all adds up to!"

"Wow!" Serena whistled when she saw the figures I'd worked out with Dad. "Do you have to pay it all?"

"Not all, but part of it. If my dad had bred her to the Jenkins' quarter horse like he planned, the ranch would pay the bills. A good fast cow pony like a quarter horse would add to our bloodlines. But since we don't know what kind of runt that mustang, Pirate, will sire, we decided the colt—or filly—would be mine, so I have to carry a share of the cost."

"That doesn't seem fair," Serena said.

"It's no secret that it was my fault Belle got out. I was the one who forgot to bolt her stall door, and I knew well enough that she'll lift the latch with her teeth if you turn your back for two seconds."

"Isn't Pirate a palomino?" Serena asked as she slipped the bridle on Bumper. "I love palominos. They're so pretty, with their blond manes and golden coats."

"There's nothing pretty about this mustang. I got

3

a look at him when we finally made it through the snowdrifts last spring to bring Belle home. He's kind of small, not more than sixteen hands, I'd guess, and covered with scars. Besides that, his head is big and blunt, and he's just a bunch of wiry muscles. No elegance to him at all, not like my Belle." I stroked her gleaming chestnut coat, a rich, coppery color.

"Where did the mustang come from?" she asked.

"No one knows. The only wild herds in Colorado are way up in the northwest. Pirate just drifted into the area one day last fall and began helping himself to some of the best mares around. The ranchers would love to get a rope on him, but he's too fast and wily."

Belle was ready so I helped Serena saddle up Bumper, then we set off on our ride. It was my favorite time of day, late afternoon, about the only time I had for myself in the summer. As a junior wrangler, I went along on the trail rides most days, to help with the guests and horses. It was a paying job, and one I enjoyed, but it wouldn't cover all the vet bills we expected. It took me a long time to save up enough to buy Belle with my earnings. I hadn't planned on this extra expense.

Wrangling took up my days, but my evenings are also pretty busy. I took on the job of coaching Jamie, our newest wrangler, with his homework.

Plus, the owners of the ranch, Anna Diamond and her husband, Andy, expected all of us staff to socialize with the guests after dinner some nights. It's fun, but it means I have little time on my own.

"I'm wondering about something," Serena said as we jogged our horses through the pine trees.

"Ask away," I said.

"You spend most of your days riding the trail with the guests. Why do you saddle up Belle and go out again once you get back?"

"Belle needs the exercise," I said. "I can't take her out on the trail every day—it would be too hard on her. Also, I have to do my share of training the other horses. But Doctor Cooper said it was important for a pregnant mare to stay fit, so I try to give her a good workout whenever she's spent the day lazing around the pasture."

"Owning a horse is a lot of responsibility, isn't it?" Serena said.

"Yup, you'll find out when you get yours. It shouldn't be too long now. You've learned to handle Bumper real well."

"He's much zippier than Sneakers, but he's a good horse. Do you think I might try jumping him soon?"

"Bumper's not a natural-born jumper. A lot of cow ponies don't care for it." I thought a moment. "You ought to try Eagle next. He likes it."

"Which one is he?"

"The blue roan Appaloosa with the spotted rump and the white blaze down his nose. But he can be a handful. I'll have to start you slow on him."

We were riding side by side, and Serena gave me

a quick glance. "You know, Chris, I was thinking ... now don't take this wrong ..."

"Take what wrong?"

"Well, you've been teaching me to ride almost all summer and I haven't paid you back, really ..."

"Your mom's given me a couple of good haircuts," I said. "You don't owe me anything."

"Yes, I do. Now, you need money to help with the vet bills and—"

"*Serena Chang!* Don't you dare say one more word! Taking money from you would be like asking someone to pay me for breathing. Drop that idea down the nearest well and fill in the hole so it never pops out again."

She sighed. "I knew you'd get mad. I'm sorry."

"I've already forgotten you said it." I sounded huffy, but I couldn't help it.

"But when will you find time to earn money another way?" she said. "Between taking the guests out, and teaching me to ride, and helping Jamie, you—" She snapped her fingers. "I just remembered! I went down into town with my brother yesterday to buy lumber, and guess what I saw?"

"Now how am I going to guess? I haven't been off the ranch since we picked up Drew's puppy. For all I know, the town washed away in the last thunderstorm and nobody thought to mention it."

She grinned. "It's still there, and so is the poster I saw. One of the churches is holding a fair in a couple of weeks and on the last day, there's going to be a big horse race—with a prize!"

"You mean a *money* prize?" I sat up real straight in the saddle.

"Five hundred dollars for the first place! Is Belle fast? Could you race her?"

"Sure she's fast. But race her? I'm not sure. I'd have to check with Doctor Cooper and see what she says."

Serena glanced down at Belle's flanks. "She doesn't even look pregnant."

"Most mares don't, not until the last couple of months, especially maiden mares like Belle, who are having their first foal."

I was talking about one thing and thinking about another: $ $ $ $ $! Those little signs were flashing in my head, blinking green—green—GREEN. "We can win it! I know we can win it!" I said.

"Wouldn't being pregnant slow Belle down?" Serena asked.

"I don't think so," I said. "I'll ask Dad. He'll know." Besides being foreman of the Double Diamond, my father was also in charge of breeding the ranch horses. Each year we raised about a dozen colts and fillies. Belle was one of them, some years back.

Up ahead, the trail branched, and I decided to head over to a spot I hadn't been to in a while. It was part of the National Forest, what they called a "Designated Wilderness Area." That meant no machines were allowed, not even a chain saw, so it's always quiet and peaceful, the way nature's supposed to be.

7

From the top of the ridge, you could see a whole long stretch of the Rocky Mountains, and down below, one of the prettiest meadows, just filled with wildflowers. It was a darn nice piece of scenery.

"Is Belle fast enough to win a race?" Serena followed me on Bumper as Belle and I led the way up the steep climb.

"I've never tried to find out, but I'll bet she is," I said. "Her mother, Sundown, won a lot of races before she went blind. That's one reason Dad rescued her from the owner, who was going to put her down. That, and her part-Arabian blood he wanted to add to our stock."

"Wait a minute!" Serena said. "You're already planning to win the five hundred dollars, but you've never raced Belle?"

"Only on the ranch. She's beaten Drew's Steamboat every time, and you know how big that gray is. He's bigger than she is, but she can whip him."

"Gosh, I'm sorry I mentioned it now," Serena said. "If Belle's never raced before . . ."

"Heck, that doesn't mean anything. I've got two weeks to get her ready." I began planning her training right then. "I'll ask Dad to let me try her against Midnight. He's a stallion, and fast. If Belle can beat him, I'll bet she can beat anyone."

Serena shook her head. "I don't know, Chris . . ." She glanced around. "Hey, where are we? I don't recognize this trail."

"We're headed for one of my favorite spots, a wilderness area. I don't come here often, but wait until you see it. It's not far now, and you're in for a real surprise."

But *I* was the one who got the surprise. We came out above the tree line, climbed up over a rocky ridge, then I reined in Belle and gasped in shock.

The entire mountain slope was crisscrossed with ugly scars. The view that always made me want to suck in my breath with wonder was spoiled by tracks that flattened the fragile plants and dug deep ruts in the earth. A huge spiderweb of pure destruction had totally ruined the mountainside and meadow.

"Bikers!" I said. "Bikers did this! Just wait until I get my hands on them!"

chapter 2

"Bikes?" Serena asked, reining in Bumper. "Bikes did this?"

The ruts scarred the slope with evil slashes and turned the meadow into a churned-up field of dead and dying wildflowers. How many animals had been hurt, or scared off, their homes wrecked?

"Trail bikes, those souped-up motor scooters." I stared at the sickening sight. "It's against the law to bring them into a Designated Wilderness Area."

"How did they get here?" Serena asked. "There isn't a road in sight."

"There's one about five miles over, behind that ridge." I pointed. "Look, you can see the path they cut to get in here." A wide line snaked through the crushed bushes and young pine trees, disappearing behind the rise.

"Why would anyone do this?" Serena asked.

"I don't know. There are plenty of legal areas to ride in, if you're the type that likes a lot of noise and speed." I beat my fist against my knee. "I'm going to report this to the rangers right away. Come on, let's go!"

We turned our horses away from the terrible sight and rode back to the Double Diamond at a good pace, neither of us saying a word. I couldn't talk, I was so full of rage and misery.

The supper gong rang as soon as we'd unsaddled and turned the horses out to pasture. Mrs. Chang was waiting to drive Serena home and I said goodbye, then caught Dad and Andy Diamond as they headed into the dining room and told them what we'd found.

"That's bad," Andy said. "Real bad. That land belongs to everyone. It's a crime that a few selfish people think they have a right to destroy it. There's too little wilderness left, as it is."

"It will take a lot of time and hard work to repair the damage, from what you described," Dad said. "If it's not done before winter, the bad weather will only make it worse. You'd better report this right now, Chris."

We went into the office and dialed the Forest Service, Andy on one phone, me on the other. The ranger took our news seriously. "We'll be up there first thing in the morning. Do you know how many bikes were involved?"

"No, sir," I said. "I didn't count the tracks, but I'd guess three or four, at least."

"Do you have any idea how long ago this occurred?" he asked.

"Some of the plants were wilted, but others were already dried up, so maybe a week or so."

"Mr. Diamond," the ranger asked, "have you heard any machines in that area recently?"

"The ranch is too far away from the area," Andy said. "But now that you ask, some of the hands working the range mentioned a noise. I'll ask them about it tonight after supper."

"We'll be out around eight in the morning," the ranger said. "Perhaps you'd like to meet us there."

"I'll come too," I said. "Even though it hurts to look at it."

"That would be a good idea, Miss Bradley. Thank you for reporting this."

We hung up and went into the dining room. Some of the guests noticed our gloom and asked about the problem. The bad news spread up and down the long tables where we all ate together, family style. Everyone had the same reaction. People come to our ranch to get away from the noise and machines, and to enjoy the pleasures of the natural world. They all showed the same mix of anger and sadness I felt. Before long, a group was asking to go along with us in the morning.

"Sorry," Dad said. "Too many horses might only

13

add to the problem, even though we're always careful to avoid causing any damage. In fact, Maggie," he said to our head wrangler, "I'm asking that the trail rides avoid that area for now. If the bikes return when you're out there, they could spook the horses and anything might happen."

"They wouldn't have the nerve to show their faces, would they?" Mr. Singer asked. He and his family had been visiting us for the last three summers and I knew him to be a hot-tempered man.

"When you're dealing with people thoughtless enough to tear up a protected area, who knows what they're capable of?" Andy said. "I agree with Bart. The area is off-limits for now."

There were a few moans and groans, but everyone respected Andy and my dad, knowing them to be fair men, with good judgment.

The rest of supper was taken up with that one topic of conversation, and it wasn't until after we ate that I remembered about the race and the chance to win five hundred sorely-needed dollars.

First I called the church and a nice lady told me the race was a quarter-mile long, in keeping with Western tradition. That mean it was a short race compared to some Eastern courses, but it judged the horse on what was needed most in cattle country—a fast start and a big burst of speed.

When a cow decides to scamper off into the brush rather than stay with the herd, you need a horse who can take off in a split second and circle around in front of her right quick. A cow who's trotting off on an adventure can look real surprised when suddenly a horse appears in her path. You can almost see her thinking, "Now, where the heck did he come from?" The next thing she knows, she's turned around, on her way back to where she belongs.

The lady from the church gave me a few more details about the race. No professional race horses or jockeys were allowed, since it was purely for fun. Only local horses were accepted, and they had to be ridden by their owners. The field was limited to nine, and already six had signed up. I had to pay a good-sized entry fee and show a vet's certificate of okay. Besides that, all I had to do was show up and win.

"Hey, Chris." Jamie poked his head into the office. "Ready for my lesson this evening?"

"Um, sure, Jamie," I said. "Just let me make one more phone call first, okay?"

"Listen, if you're busy, Maggie can coach me tonight," he said. "You look like you've got a lot on your mind. Is it the bike damage you found today?"

"Yes, that, plus I want to enter Belle in a race and I need to ask Doctor Cooper if it's okay, with her carrying a foal."

"A race?" Jamie lit up. "Which one?"

So I told him about the vet bills and the church fair and the prize money.

"Then don't worry about the lesson tonight. I'll be fine with Maggie." Jamie gave me his handsome grin and left.

I dialed the vet's number and Dr. Cooper herself

15

answered. In the background I could hear her three-year-old arguing with his daddy about eating all the peas on his plate.

"I don't see any reason why Belle can't run a short race," she said after I asked my question. I left out the part about needing the prize money to pay her vet bills—no sense worrying her over it. "She's in great shape, and if you train her properly, working her up gradually, she should be fine."

"That's super," I said. "Dad will help. He knows all about horses."

"Great," she said, then added, "I'll be at the fair, rooting for you and Belle."

"Don't worry," I said. "If I decide to enter her, she'll win."

Dr. Cooper laughed. "That's what makes horse racing."

I was looking for Dad when I came across Drew playing Monopoly with the Singer kids in the lounge. Drew is a year older than me, going into seventh grade, but we've been best pals forever, growing up on the ranch together. His parents are Andy and Anna Diamond, and his actual name is Andrew John Diamond the Fourth.

Drew tossed the dice and landed on "Go Directly to Jail."

"Not again!" he muttered, throwing giggling Sarah a dark look. "And don't you dare laugh, Miss Silly Singer. I still own Boardwalk with two hotels and you're about to land on it."

16

She stuck out her tongue at him, then rolled the dice. Boardwalk.

"Hah! Who's laughing now?" Drew crowed, raking in the money she slowly handed over. He thought he was all grown up when he was hanging around with his guy friends, but I noticed he still enjoyed winning at a kid's game.

"Hi, Elephant Baby," I said, stooping to pat Drew's puppy who lay beside the table waiting for someone to drop a pretzel. "It looks like you've grown a couple more inches since breakfast."

"Don't call him 'Elephant,'" Drew said. "His name is Star and you know it."

"That's a dumb name for a dog," Sarah Singer said. "I think you should call him 'Baby.' He's so cute." She rubbed the puppy's fuzzy black fur and he licked her hand, his chubby tail thumping.

"*Baby* is a dumb name for a dog," Sarah's brother, Jon, said. "I think you should call him 'Moose.' My mom says with paws as big as his, that's the size he'll grow to."

"Moose! I like that," I said.

"He's my dog and I'll call him what I want," Drew said. "It's your turn, Jon. Roll the dice."

"Drew, I'm looking for Dad," I said. "Have you seen him?"

"I think he's out by the pool," he said. "Talking to Mrs. Morris. Again." He winked at me.

I walked away, frowning. What the heck did that wink mean?

Mrs. Morris was a widow who used to stay with

17

us when her husband was alive. They were a real nice couple, one of our favorites, and we were all sorry when he died in a car crash two years ago. She didn't come last year, but was making up for it by staying a whole month this summer. All our guests visit for at least a week, sometimes longer. That way you get to know each other.

I stopped in the doorway leading out to the pool. A few people were swimming in the heated water, but I knew as soon as they got out they'd scurry to their cabins to change. In the Rockies, it gets too chilly at night to hang around in a wet bathing suit.

Dad and Mrs. Morris were sitting at a table near the far end of the pool, talking and watching the early moon rising. The mountain peaks poked up against the sky, stained red with the sunset. As always, I thought there couldn't be a better place to live than in the Colorado Rockies.

I wanted to rush over and ask Dad about using Midnight to help train Belle for the race, but something about the way he sat listening to Mrs. Morris made me stay put. His face looked . . . different. He was my same old Dad, but he gave off a . . . new . . . feeling.

My parents had been divorced a long time. Mom hated the ranch, but when she married my father and had me, she stuck around until I was six to take care of me. Then she left to pick up her career. She's a country-western singer, and she's going to make it big one day soon.

18

She called every Sunday night, and we talked lots of other times too, so I knew all about her life. We were both sure all she needed was that one big break, the one important star or record producer to hear her, and *Bam!* she'd be off to Nashville, fame, and fortune.

Meanwhile, I'd never seen Dad pay much attention to other ladies. I was sure he still loved my mom too much to bother.

At least, I'd been sure—until now. *Now,* watching him with Mrs. Morris, *now* I wasn't sure at all.

chapter 3

Watching Dad and Mrs. Morris together, so many feelings raced through me I couldn't keep up with them all. A purple flash of surprise, a big green jolt of jealousy, a red-coal glow of anger, a deep blue plunge of sorrow. And weaving in and out through it all, a sunshine-yellow ribbon of pleasure due to the happiness I saw in Dad's eyes.

Before I could turn away, Dad spotted me. "Chris, come on over. Amanda was just asking me about growing up on a ranch, and you're an expert on the subject."

Wishing I could go off by myself and sort through all my feelings first, I slowly walked over to their table and sat in a chair across from Mrs. Morris. "What is it you want to know, ma'am?"

"Oh, all sorts of things," she said with a smile. "I grew up in the suburbs, with a father who took a train to work every weekday, leaving at seven in the morning and not getting home until seven at night. He mowed the lawn or raked leaves on Saturdays, and read the *New York Times* on Sundays. I was just telling your father that your life must be so different, having him around all the time and working side by side with him. I envy you."

She envied *me*? Mrs. Morris, with her shiny golden hair and perfect fingernails, her designer blue jeans and three-hundred-dollar boots? She could go out on an overnight pack trip and come back looking like she'd just stepped out of a beauty parlor.

What was I supposed to say? "Well, it's not a bad life, I guess."

"Do you miss living in town and seeing your friends more often?" she asked.

"No, ma'am. I've got all the friends I need right here. I've got Belle, and Drew, and Serena, and there are always guests around to keep you company."

She laughed. "I notice you listed your horse first. You really are a Westerner, aren't you?"

I felt my ears tingle red with embarrassment. What else would I be, born and raised in the Rockies? "I guess so, ma'am." I tried to sound polite.

"I'm sorry, Chris," she said quickly. "I meant that as a compliment. You know I love the ranch and the mountains, the people, the horses and the cattle— everything about the place. When I go back to Connecticut, it takes me weeks to get over missing the Double Diamond and this way of life."

Was that a hint? I wondered. Was she maybe planning *not* to leave again? Was she thinking of staying for good? With Dad? And me?

"You've only been here in the summer, Amanda," Dad said. "It's a different story in the winter. It can get so cold it hurts to breathe, and the snowdrifts can reach right up over the ranch house windows at times."

I watched his face carefully. His words were discouraging, but the softness around his eyes made me think he was hoping she didn't care how bad the winters got.

"But people pay a fortune to come out here for the skiing," she said. "Aspen, Vail . . . why, half the people I know fly out over Christmas and during the school winter vacation to ski."

"Vail and Aspen are resort towns, with restaurants and shops and night life," Dad said. "Living and working on a ranch is very different."

"Yes, I'm sure that's true," she said quietly, their eyes fixed on each other.

I stood up. I'd heard—and seen—enough. "Um, Dad, I need to talk to you, later. Whenever you get back to the cabin."

Dad glanced at his watch. "It's a little early to turn in, Chris."

"I have reading to do," I said. "Good night, Mrs. Morris. See you later, Dad."

I share a log cabin with Dad, set off a distance from the main ranch house, in its own little grove of aspen trees. It's small but cheery, with red-checked curtains Mom made before she left us, big comfy chairs, and a fireplace, of course.

Also, there are books. Lots and lots of books, mainly about horses and ranching. Some Mom sent me—she visits every used-book store she comes across in her travels from one singing job to another, and usually manages to dig out a horse story I haven't yet read. Other books belonged to Dad, to help him in his job of ranch foreman and horse breeder.

I was glad to drag down a heavy book on racing to shift my mind away from Mrs. Morris. The situation would have to be thought about, but I felt like putting it off for a while.

The first fact I learned was that two weeks was a real short time to get a race horse ready. The book talked about months, and even years. Well, I decided, I didn't have that kind of time so I'd just have to make do. Besides, they were talking about fancy Thoroughbreds, who are known to be high-strung and fussy. My Belle is a solid, down-to-earth horse who knows what work is and runs a good hard gallop every day of her life.

I was reading about special feeds when Dad came home. "They sure coddle those race horses, don't they?" I asked him as he hung up his hat.

"What do you mean?" he asked, working his boots off.

Prize-Winning Horse, Maybe

I showed him the book cover. "All this special food—hot mash, and add this, add that. Do I have to do that if I'm going to race Belle?"

"Whoa," he said. "Back up and start over."

So I told him my plans to win the five hundred dollars. "Belle is fast enough, isn't she? She always beats Drew's Steamboat."

"She's fast at short distances, like the quarter mile," Dad agreed, sitting down and propping his legs up on the hassock. "And her mother won a lot of races in her time. You might have a chance with her, but I wouldn't count on winning, Chris."

"Oh, if I enter, I'm going to win all right. Can I try her out against Midnight tomorrow? Your stallion is the only real competition for her we have on the ranch."

"I'm not sure," Dad said. "Midnight hasn't been ridden for a few days and he's a bit on the frisky side. Why don't you let me take him out on the range and give him a good workout to settle him down before we try it?"

"Oh, please, Dad. I have to know right away if Belle can beat him. No sense spending money on the entry fee if she can't win. The lady at the church said six horses are already signed up and they only allow nine total, so I have to decide right away if it's worth it."

Dad rubbed his forehead, thinking. "Okay, I'll ride Midnight when we go out to meet the rangers in the morning. After a good long hike to the wilderness area, he might be quiet enough."

"That's great. Then we can race Belle against him on the way home." I snapped the book shut and stood up. "Time for bed. It's almost nine o'clock."

"I'll be along shortly."

"You'll be sorry you delayed when the alarm goes off at five." I gave him back the very words he used on me when I was tempted to stay up late.

"I know." He waved me off. "And, Chris . . ."

Stopping in my bedroom doorway, I turned back. "Yes?"

"About Amanda—Mrs. Morris. I . . ." He kept his eyes on the cold, empty fireplace. "I don't want you to worry. We, uh, well . . . we're just friends. Friends, that's all."

"Sure, Dad, I know that. Friends."

He sighed. "Your mama has been gone a long time, Chris. Five years. And sometimes a man needs . . . well, a little female company. A lady, just to talk to, you know."

"Don't worry, Dad, I understand. Good night." I closed the door to my room, wondering who he was trying to convince. Me—or himself?

The morning chores take a good two hours. We have to bring the trail horses in from pasture, clean their hooves of small stones or anything that might make them go lame, check them for swollen legs or cuts, brush them, water and feed them, and of course, saddle up. When you're talking about a couple dozen horses, even with all the wranglers working, it takes a fair amount of time.

That day, Drew and Maggie took over some of my load because I had to leave early with Dad and Andy to get to the wilderness area to meet the rangers at 8:00 A.M. It was a cloudy morning, kind of chilly, and I was hoping it wouldn't rain.

Dad had a job with Midnight, who, after a few days of rest, was feeling plenty sparky. Stallions can be a handful, and Dad was the only one who could really manage him. But by the time we'd climbed to the top of the ridge, Midnight had finally settled down some. We rode down to the meadow where the rangers were studying the bike tracks.

"What a mess," Andy said after he made introductions.

"Yes, sir, it's a lot of destruction," one of the rangers, Officer Adams, said. "We're especially worried about the mountainside. Heavy rains, or the snow of winter, can cause a lot of erosion if the damage isn't repaired. All those ruts will turn into little gullies. Without plants to hold the soil in place, the water will wash away the tundra in no time."

"How can people be so stupid?" I asked. "Can't they read signs?" I pointed to one in plain view, stating clear as day that this was a Designated Wilderness Area.

"Some people think only of themselves," Officer Adams said. "We figure there were four bikers, just as you guessed, Miss Bradley. We'll post more signs along the trail they cut coming in from the highway."

"Can't you do anything else to stop them?" I asked.

"Well, we'll roll a few logs across the path, hoping to slow them down, and we'll send patrols by on a regular basis. This might be a one-time thing though, so with luck, they won't be back."

"Is there anything we can do?" Dad asked.

"You can help us pin down the time, for one thing," Officer Adams said. "Mr. Diamond, did you question the hands who said they'd heard a noise in this area?"

"Yes," Andy said. "It was five days ago, around noon. My range land is over on the other side of the ridge, and the men said they heard a distant buzzing. They weren't sure where it was coming from, and didn't have time to investigate at any rate. It was after that big windstorm, and we had fences down all over the place."

Officer Adams nodded. "I'll send a crew out to work on some of these ruts. It might also help if you people kept an ear out for the bikers. Call us if you suspect they've come back."

"We can do more than that," Dad said. "I've asked our wranglers to keep the guests away from here, but one of us could make it a practice to stop by every so often, just to keep an eye on the area."

"That would help beef up our patrols. Thank you, sir."

Prize-Winning Horse, Maybe

Officer Adams left to join the other rangers, who were replanting the roots of young pine seedlings that weren't quite dead yet.

We rode back in silence for a while. My stomach was churning with anger, thinking of people who were so selfish they didn't care what they hurt.

"Cheer up, Chris," Dad said. "They probably won't be back."

"Yeah, but then they'll tear up some other pretty spot instead. Why can't they keep to the areas set aside for trail bikes?"

"Or, if they want to explore new country," Dad said, "why don't they learn to ride? A well-managed horse with a responsible rider isn't destructive. And speaking of well-mannered horses, are you ready to find out how fast Belle can run this morning?"

I was happy to turn my thoughts to the race. We'd just come out of the trees at the edge of a meadow, and there was lots of open space in front of us. "I sure am. The thing is, though, Midnight is all rested up and Belle has been exercised a lot recently."

"That will give him an edge," Dad admitted. "Provided he doesn't toss me off instead. But at least we can get a timing on Belle." He pulled out a stopwatch and handed it to Andy. "I'd guess that spruce tree is about a quarter mile off, wouldn't you say, Andy?"

"About," Andy agreed. "I'll ride over and be waiting at the finish line." He trotted off.

29

Then I had one more thought. "Midnight will have another edge because he's a stallion, won't he?"

"Not necessarily." Dad dismounted and checked Belle's girth to be sure it was good and tight, then did the same for Midnight. "In the wild, it's actually the top mare who leads the herd. She's the one who decides when and where to go. The stallion usually brings up the rear, to protect his ladies from danger that might be stalking the herd from behind. So unless Midnight has a competitive streak I haven't noticed, he's unlikely to have an advantage just because he's a male."

"But isn't it usually the stallions who win the big races, like the Kentucky Derby?" I asked.

"Not always. Fillies have won lots of big races. But you're talking about Thoroughbreds, who have the racing instinct born into them. A good cow pony like Midnight knows how to cut a cow from a herd, how to round up a stray, how to keep the tension on the rope while his rider ties up a calf. *Those* are the instincts born into him."

"And Belle has some racing blood," I said with relief. "Since it's only local horses competing in the church fair race, maybe she'll have the edge over the other cow ponies."

"Maybe so." Dad remounted Midnight. "All set?"

"Yup." I patted Belle's neck. "We're ready, aren't we, Belle?"

She bobbed her head and snorted. She's so smart, I could almost guarantee she understands English.

30

Midnight was dancing around a good bit, impatient with our talk. Dad had to take a couple of seconds to settle him in place.

"On three," Dad said. "Ready? One . . . two . . . three!"

My heels touched Belle's flank and she sprang forward like a jackrabbit. In two paces, she was going at a full run.

Midnight was beside us, shaking his head like he didn't care for Dad's signals, but he was running fast, his head even with her shoulder.

"Go, Belle!" I whooped with joy.

She picked up speed, but Midnight drew even with her. As soon as she caught sight of him, her neck stretched out and she began to fly over the ground.

She pulled ahead. Midnight dropped back. Then he pulled even again. Belle wasn't having it. Her hooves pounded double time. Midnight fell behind.

We flashed past the spruce tree.

It was over. Already. It seemed to take only seconds to run a quarter mile.

Belle didn't want to stop. As long as Midnight was chasing her, she was going to keep racing. Finally I managed to turn her away after Dad pulled Midnight off in the other direction.

We met back at the spruce tree, both horses panting with happiness.

Andy showed me the stopwatch. "Darn good time you made."

Dad glanced at it and whistled. "Not bad. But

more than that, Chris, she showed the instinct. She wasn't going to let Midnight get in front of her."

"You mean—" I grinned so wide a fly could have flown in and out of my mouth and I wouldn't have noticed.

"Yup. You've got a race horse there."

chapter 4

I needed to help to spy out the competition—and fast, before the last racing spaces were taken. Now that we knew Belle could run, we had to know who she was up against, and how good they were, before I plunked down my hard-earned money for the entry fee.

Drew and Serena volunteered to take the first step the next morning so I could spend the time training Belle.

Getting into town was easier than it used to be before the Changs bought the Lazy B. Serena's family was doing so much rebuilding and repair on their ranch that her father or one of her brothers went down the mountain for supplies almost every day.

Prize-Winning Horse, Maybe

Serena's brother, Tommy, dropped her and Drew off at the church on his way to the lumberyard. The lady I'd spoken to, Mrs. Wilber, had promised to give them a look at the entry list. I spent some time working with Belle, then went to our cabin with Dad to wait for Drew's planned call. At eleven, he rang me from a pay phone and I snatched up the receiver.

"There's only one space left," Drew reported. "Eight horses are signed up now. If you're going to enter Belle, this is your last chance."

Dad was standing beside me, ready to check over the list as Drew gave me the names. As a breeder, Dad knew an awful lot of horses in the area.

"Read 'em out," I told Drew, crossing my fingers.

"Patches, a piebald pinto owned by the Lonesome Pine Ranch," I repeated to Dad after Drew told me.

Dad nodded. "A good cow pony, but not real fast."

"Jacks Are Wild, a gray Appaloosa owned by Judy Stine," I repeated.

"Old Jackie," Dad said. "He was a great horse in his prime, but he must be sixteen or seventeen years old by now."

"Sunburst, a palomino owned by Laurie and Lance Holtz."

"Nice horse," Dad said, "but I'd say he'd be better off in a longer race. He's got staying power, but he's not real quick out of the gate."

"Bucket, a roan Appaloosa owned by J. Cummings."

Dad shook his head. "I don't know him."

"Make a mark by Bucket, Drew," I said. "We'll have to scout him out." I listened a moment, then told Dad, "Pilgrim, a dapple gray owned by the Harmon Ranch."

"Hmm," Dad said. "He might be trouble. I saw him compete in the rodeo last year. He's sired by the Jenkins' quarter horse, and he's fast."

"Check off Pilgrim, too," I told Drew. "Dad thinks he might be competition, so we'd better take a look at him."

"Oh, no," Drew groaned. "You're not going to like this. Skittles, a bay owned by Chuck Jenkins."

"Shoot me!" I shouted. "That's Pilgrim's sire and the horse that Dad wanted to father Belle's foal!"

Dad took the phone from me. "Are you sure Chuck is entering Skittles?" he asked Drew. "The horse turns out great foals, but I always thought he was too wild to handle in a crowd."

Dad listened to Drew, then nodded and gave the phone back to me. "Chuck must be gambling he can control him. The last time he tried to race Skittles, maybe three years ago, that stallion ran clean off the rack two seconds into the race. But if he behaves, he'll give Belle a run for her money."

I felt glum, but I told Drew, "Go on."

"Athena, a buckskin owned by W.W. Winthrop," Drew said, and I passed it on to Dad.

"I've never seen her," Dad said.

"Warpaint, a skewbald pinto owned by the Learner family," Drew said. "That name sounds familiar."

36

"I know him!" I said. "He's one of *our* colts!"

"Which one is it?" Dad asked.

"Warpaint," I said. "I remember the night he was born! I was only about seven, and you woke me up and took me to the stables because I'd been complaining that foals are always born at night and I never saw them arrive."

"I remember too," Dad said. "I'll never forget the way you looked when that little fella made his appearance. It was like I'd just given you the sun, the moon, and the stars, all wrapped up in one scrawny little package of pinto colt."

"Hey," Drew said. "Stop talking to each other on my dime. That's the list. Should I enter Belle or not?"

"Wait a second! Let me talk it over with Dad." I put my hand over the mouthpiece, for no real reason except habit. "Let's go over what we've got. Two unknown horses, three who are probably no problem, Pilgrim, who's fast, and Skittles, who may not stay on the track, but if he does, he's trouble. What about Warpaint, Dad?"

"His mama turns out real nice trail horses," Dad said, "and I've never thought of Warpaint as anything other than a good, reliable ride. We sold him to the Learners for their kids. Unless he grew up into a surprise, I don't see how he can win."

"I'll bet I know why he's entered," I said. "Susan Learner is in my class at school, and I think she just wants a chance to be in a race. She's an okay rider, but nothing special. Let's put Warpaint in the 'no problem' group."

A distant voice was shouting at me. I put the phone to my ear. *"Chris! What do you want me to do?"* Drew was yelling. *"I'm almost out of change for this dumb phone!"*

"I can hear you," I said. "Take it easy." I looked at Dad. He nodded. "Drew, go ahead and give Mrs. Wilber my money. Looks like Belle only has four horses to beat, maybe less if the ones Dad doesn't know aren't any good. Besides, I'll bet she can win no matter how fast they are. She has the racing instinct in her."

"I know, I know," Drew said. "You've only said that about three thousand times since she beat Midnight yesterday. Okay, anything else?"

"Get the addresses of the two Dad doesn't know, Bucket and Athena, and if they're anywhere nearby, see if you can't talk Tommy into driving you over to take a peek at them. Then report back to me."

"Yes, sir, General Chris, sir. You can't see me, but I'm saluting, sir!" He hung up.

Well, gee, someone had to organize this racing business, didn't they?

The next morning I got a brilliant idea. If I rode Belle out on the trail with the advanced riders, I could run her fast and hard from time to time, even race her against our best horses. That way I could continue her training while I worked.

Then I'd have late afternoon to scout out Belle's competition with Dad. Usually Drew and I, being only junior wranglers, helped with the beginner groups but to my pleased surprise, Dad okayed my plan.

The main drawback was that Mrs. Morris was an advanced rider, so it meant spending the days with her, but that turned out not to be too bad. She didn't try to cozy up to me or anything, just treated me the way she always had, friendly and pleasant, like she was with everyone.

Bucket, one of the unknown competitors, lived just outside of town, but Athena lived far to the south, so Drew and Serena had only seen Bucket. They reported that the Appaloosa was around sixteen hands and well formed, but he'd just been grazing in the pasture so they hadn't seen him in action.

Dad had done some calling around and found out Bucket's owner was Joan Cummings, a newcomer from the East. She'd bought him as a pleasure horse, but before that, he'd been working cattle up in Montana. So far, that was all we knew.

After we returned from the trail that afternoon, I finished up my horses quickly and ran to the main ranch house, where I planned to meet Dad. I whipped around the corner then skidded to a halt.

Dad was waiting in our station wagon. And so was Mrs. Morris.

To say I was disappointed was like saying the Rocky Mountains are only sand dunes. Aside from wanting to check out Belle's competition, I'd been looking forward to having Dad all to myself for a time. It's not easy to share your father with an entire ranchful of duties and chores, plus all the guests who enjoyed his company so much.

"Ready, Chris?" Dad called.

I put one boot in front of the other, forcing myself to walk over to the car. "Um, sure."

"Hop in, then." He turned on the engine.

I tried to open the door to the backseat, but it felt like my hands had suddenly grown into big, thick gloves. I fumbled with the handle.

Mrs. Morris was watching me. "Bart," she said, "I've changed my mind. I'd rather stay here. You and Chris don't need me, and I just remembered I . . . I have something to do."

"Amanda," Dad said, "I thought we decided this was a good time for the three of us to—"

"We were wrong," she said quickly, getting out of the car. "Sit up here with your father, Chris." She left the door open and hurried up the porch steps. "I'll see you when you get back. And I hope that horse, Bucket, turns out to be a scrawny old nag!"

I waited until she went inside before I climbed into the front seat beside Dad.

"Now what was that all about?" he asked.

I shrugged.

"Women! Always changing their minds." He put the car in gear and started down the drive.

I said nothing. Inside, I was torn in two. Mrs. Morris knew right away how I felt and she didn't take more than two seconds to set things right. That showed what a nice lady she was—and how smart. Still, I resented her for even thinking of coming along in the first place.

Unless it was all Dad's idea.

I decided I didn't want to know the answer to that question.

"How did Belle do today?" Dad asked.

I heaved a sigh of relief and put Mrs. Morris straight out of my mind. "I raced her against Mr. Singer on Windjammer and she won, of course. You can see it growing in her, that need to stay out front."

"Good." Dad nodded. "Did she bolt the gate again?"

"Only once." That was Belle's main problem. She was so eager to race that sometimes she'd take off before I gave her the signal. If that happened at the fair, it would be a false start, and if she did it more than once, she might be disqualified—chucked right off the track by the officials.

"Well, keep working on it." Dad turned onto the road that led to town, more than an hour away.

We went on discussing Belle's training until we pulled up in front of Bucket's place. It was an ordinary, smallish house, attached to a pasture about half an acre in size. The Appaloosa was grazing away, and a lady was coming out of the garage, carrying a couple of grocery bags.

"Evening, ma'am," Dad said getting out of the car. "Can I help you with those?"

"Why . . . um." She looked real startled.

"I'm Bart Bradley," Dad said, tipping his hat. "I'm the foreman at the Double Diamond Dude Ranch, and this is my daughter, Crystal."

Darn, there he went again, I thought as I hopped out of the car. He kept forgetting and calling me by my real name.

"Uh, hello . . ." She still seemed a bit spooked.

"Are you Ms. Cummings?" Dad asked. "I believe your horse and my daughter's are both entered in the church fair race, and we were curious to see what our competition might be like."

"Oh, of course." She began to relax a little. "I'm sorry. I didn't mean to appear rude. I haven't been out here long, and back East we get a little nervous when a stranger . . . well, I'm sorry. Yes, I'm Joan Cummings."

"I understand, ma'am." Dad took the grocery bags from her. "The East strikes me as being a particularly unfriendly place to live."

"That's one reason I moved West." She smiled and unlocked her front door. She was of a medium age, not old but not young either, and she wore a business-type suit, so I figured she must work in an office.

We followed her into the house and Dad put the grocery bags on the kitchen counter.

"Would you like a cup of coffee?" she asked.

"Thank you, no, ma'am," Dad said. "We can't stay long."

"So we'll be racing against each other," Ms. Cummings said to me. "Tell me about your horse, Crystal."

"Call me just plain Chris," I said, then told her a little about Belle. I didn't brag about her racing instincts though, or her speed—why give away our secrets?

Ms. Cummings gazed out the window at Bucket in the pasture. "I'm not expecting to win the race," she said. "The main reason I entered was to meet people, since I'm new in town."

Right then she gave Dad one of Those Looks. You could see her sizing him up, and liking what she saw. I was used to it, because a lot of the lady guests who came to the Double Diamond did the same thing. Dad isn't bad looking, for a cowboy whose idea of getting all dressed up was to put on a clean pair of jeans and a fresh-ironed shirt. He never seemed to notice Those Looks though, and went on being polite and friendly, not favoring anyone in particular.

Until Mrs. Morris returned this summer.

I shoved the thought away and tried to tune in on what Ms. Cummings was saying. ". . . and I'm so used to riding with an English saddle, I forget and try to post the trot on poor Bucket. He doesn't know what to make of me, I'm sure. But I'm determined to learn Western ways, in everything, not only riding. When in Rome . . ."

". . . do as the Romans do," Dad finished for her. "With that attitude, you'll get on well out here."

"Thank you." She was real pleased. "Anyway,

Crystal—I mean, Chris—Bucket's a fast little horse, but I won't push him too hard. I've only had him a few weeks and we're just getting to know each other. As I said, I entered for the fun of it, and to meet people."

"I'm sure you'll do well, ma'am," I said.

Outside, something caught Bucket's attention. He lifted his head to listen, then jogged over to the fence to see whatever was happening down the road. I watched the way he moved and noticed his neck and withers were thick, giving him a short stride. He' have to take extra steps to keep up with Belle's long, gliding stride.

Once we were back in the car headed home, I said to Dad, "We can add Bucket to the 'no problem' list, I think." I told him about my observation.

"You're getting pretty sharp, Chris," he said. "I wondered if you'd pick that up. Plus, with an owner who doesn't care if she wins or not, he's got two strikes against him."

I was pleased, but I also was worried. So far, the race was looking too easy. I had a feeling that we might spot real trouble when we checked out the other unknown horse, Athena, and Pilgrim, the gray who had so impressed Dad at the rodeo last year.

As it turned out, I was right to worry.

chapter 5

"What's the matter, Chris?" Serena asked. "You haven't heard a word I've said. Is something wrong?"

It was the next afternoon and she was keeping me company on the front-porch steps while we waited for Dad to get back from the range.

Drew had promised to give Serena a riding lesson while I was gone. With the race coming up, I didn't have much time to teach her, since I was busy training Belle. She said she didn't mind, but I noticed she was real pleased when Drew offered to help out this afternoon.

"Nothing's wrong," I said. Serena was a good friend, but I was carrying a heavy load and I didn't want to burden her with it.

"Come on, Chris, you can tell me. I can keep a secret." She pushed her shiny dark hair back from her face. "Please. I know you're worried about something. Is it the race?"

"No, Belle's coming along nicely." I glanced at her, wondering if I should—or could—spit it out.

"Is it the bikers? They haven't come back, have they?"

"Nope, no sign of them, and Officer Adams said he hasn't received any more reports."

"That's good." Serena looked off in the distance at the mountain slopes. "Is your father the problem?"

"How did you know?" I was so surprised my mouth dropped open like a trap door.

"Drew said your dad and Mrs. Morris are . . . spending time together." Her voice was real soft. "I tried to think how I'd feel about that if I was in your place. I probably wouldn't like it."

"That's just it," I said. "I can't decide *how* to feel about it. Half of me says that Mom's been gone for years, and I know she'll never come back here to live. She and Dad are divorced—that's over and done with a long time ago. So why shouldn't Dad be . . . talking to . . . other ladies?"

"Mrs. Morris seems like a nice person."

"That's part of the problem!" I jumped up and stalked over to the hitching post. "She's *real* nice. Not fakey-nice and sugary-sweet, to win me over. But deep-down, decent-nice, if you know what I mean."

46

"What's wrong with that?" Serena asked, following me.

"How can you hate a person like that?" I pounded my fist against the post. "But that's what I want to do. I want to hate her."

"Why?"

"Because ... because ..." I dropped my eyes, studying the dust on my boots. "Because I want to keep Dad all to myself. I don't want to ... share him. Now, isn't that the dumbest thing you ever heard?"

Serena smiled. "No, it's not the dumbest. It's probably the most *honest* thing I've ever heard. That's what I like about you, Chris. You never mess around. You tell it like it is, even stuff that's hard to deal with. And having your dad ... interested ... in a lady, that's got to be really tough. All these years it's been just the two of you."

"Yeah, and I figured it'd go on being just the two of us ... I don't know why." I looked up toward the barn. Dad had just ridden in and was turning his horse over to one of the wranglers. He'd be along any minute. "And what makes it even harder, is him. When he's with Mrs. Morris, he's different ... happy, I guess you'd call it."

"And you want him to be happy," Serena said quietly.

"Of course I do! What kind of mean-spirited rattlesnake wouldn't want her own father to be happy? But why does his being happy have to make me *not* happy?"

47

"I see what you mean." She watched Dad coming toward us. "It's a problem, all right."

"Hi, girls," Dad called as he came near. "Howdy, Serena. Are you coming with us today?"

"No, sir." She shook her head. "Drew's going to watch me work Bumper and see if he thinks I'm ready to move up to Eagle. I want to learn to jump, and Chris says Eagle likes it."

"That he does, but he's a handful." Dad pulled the keys to the station wagon out of his pocket. "Do you think you're ready for him?"

"Not yet, but I hope to be soon." She picked up her cowboy hat that she'd left on the steps and put it on, getting ready to head up to the barn.

"You're a sensible girl, Serena," Dad said, opening the car door. "You're willing to take one step at a time. You'll turn into an excellent rider someday soon."

She blushed with pleasure, then said good-bye and headed for the barn.

"What's the plan?" Dad asked me as we got in the station wagon.

"We should have time to look at both Pilgrim and Athena," I said. "I checked with Mrs. Wilber again and found out that the mare is stabled not far from the Harmon ranch, even though her owner lives way south of town."

"Okay," Dad said. "Let's go by the boarding stable first, then stop in at the ranch. That way we'll catch the Harmons when their working day is over. We probably won't see Pilgrim in action, but you

48

can tell a lot about a horse just by looking, as you demonstrated yesterday. Also, George tends to like to talk, so maybe we can pick up some clues that way."

"Sounds good," I agreed.

All during the long drive down the mountain, I kept thinking about bringing up the subject of Mrs. Morris, but I veered away from it. I had a lot to figure out in my own mind before I was ready to discuss it.

Instead, Dad and I talked horses, and he told me stories about his rodeo days, when he'd won a bunch of prizes and almost as many broken bones. Life on the rodeo circuit can be tough.

We found the Gold Mine Stables with no problem. Dad knew the lady who ran it—sometimes I think he knows everyone in Colorado—and she was happy to point out the buckskin, Athena. The stable owner liked to talk, and she told us W.W. Winthrop—usually called Wally—was in high school, hadn't been riding long, and had more money than horse sense, in her opinion.

She and Dad moved on to other subjects, so I went over to take a look at Athena. Wally Winthrop was exercising her in the pasture set aside for practice. I leaned on the fence and watched them.

The buckskin was a good-sized mare, probably sixteen-plus hands to Belle's fifteen. At first glance, she didn't impress me much. Her height came from her large body, and I guessed her legs weren't much longer than Belle's, giving her about the same

49

length stride. But under the deep chest and wide hindquarters were legs that could really run.

This became clear when another horse entered the pasture and Wally Winthrop challenged the other rider to race. Dad came over to join me just as they set up the "starting gate"—a couple of jump rails they pulled into position.

At the signal, Athena leaped forward and flew across the grass at breakneck speed, her hooves churning up the ground. She beat the other horse by three lengths, at least.

"Wow, Dad, she's going to be some competition, isn't she?" I said.

"Looks like it." He squinted into the sun, watching as Athena slowed and her owner brought her around, headed toward us. "But take at look at her rider."

Wally Winthrop had a thin, sharp face—kind of handsome if you like that type—and was built lean like a good rider, but he was fighting to stay in control of his horse. He kept sawing at the mare's mouth with the reins and she tossed her head, trying to shake the bit loose.

"Athena, you're a bad horse," he said as they went past us. "Now cut that out, Athena. Behave yourself."

At the sound of his voice, her ears went flat against her head and she flicked her tail so hard you could actually hear it whistle as it slashed the air. That was one angry horse.

"She's too much for him," Dad said.

"She doesn't like him," I said. "And I don't blame her."

"He needs to find a horse at his level, one he can learn on," Dad said. "But that's a nice mare. With the right rider, she could really be something."

"She's awful fast," I agreed. "If someone else rode her in the race, Belle would have a hard time winning."

"Athena might still be real competition though," Dad said. "She loves to run, you can see that. She might be able to do it in spite of her owner."

"Belle can beat her," I said, but I didn't feel real sure I meant it.

We drove over to the Harmon's ranch to see Pilgrim. About a dozen horses were in the pasture beside the driveway, and Dad pointed him out. He looked pretty as a postcard. His dapple-gray coat shone in the late sunshine and he held his well-shaped head erect, watching us go past with bright, alert eyes.

"He's looking better than ever," Dad said.

"He's trouble, isn't he?" I asked.

"Could be, could be . . ."

Mrs. Harmon was glad to see us and insisted on giving us iced tea. We'd just settled on the porch when Mr. Harmon came in from the barn.

"Bart Bradley, how have you been? Good to see you." Mr. Harmon was a short, wiry man, gray-haired and grizzled.

"How's it going, George?" Dad shook his hand. "You know my daughter, Crystal."

"Call me just plain Chris." I sighed. How many times did I have to remind him?

We settled down and they talked about this and that, then finally Dad got around to explaining the reason for our visit. "I remember Pilgrim from the rodeo, and my daughter wanted to take a look at him."

"Smart girl," Mr. Harmon said. "It pays to know what you're up against. Tell me about your mare."

I told him, again leaving out the part about her racing instincts and speed. I finished by saying, "She's never run in a real race before, so we don't know how she'll do, but I wanted to give her a try."

Mr. Harmon nodded. "If she's anything like her mother, she could be fast. I remember when you acquired Sundown, Bart. There were some who laughed because you were willing to take on a blind mare, but I hear some of her colts and fillies have turned out to be real nice."

"Not bad," Dad said. "Not bad at all."

In truth, he was hopping proud of every one of them. But of course it wouldn't be polite to say so.

"So you want to see Pilgrim, do you, Chris?" Mr. Harmon said. "Come on."

We followed him down to the top of the pasture. The gray was at the far end, near a creek that ran through the trees. Mr. Harmon whistled and Pilgrim came running.

That horse could move! He flowed over the grass, all sleek strength, a beautiful thing to see. I couldn't help admiring him, even while my heart was sinking, thinking about Belle being up against him.

"He's really something," I said as he came up to the fence. No sense in not being honest.

"He's a good cow pony." Mr. Harmon scratched his mane and Pilgrim almost purred with delight. "And fast," he added, not bragging. Just stating a fact.

"Well, sir," I said with the best smile I could dig up, "I'll guess we'll find out who's the fastest for sure a week from Sunday."

"That's the spirit, Chris." Mr. Harmon winked at me. "And that's what makes horse racing."

Dr. Cooper had said the same thing, but I still wasn't sure what it meant.

We went on talking for a while, then left, stopping in town for burgers and fries, since supper would be over by the time we got back to the ranch. While we ate, we agreed to put aside all thoughts of the race. Instead, Dad told stories of the ranches he'd worked on, the people he'd met, the horses he remembered. It's awful nice to go out to dinner with your father once in a while. Just the two of you.

I was still feeling relaxed the next morning when Belle and I set out with the advanced riders, which of course included Mrs. Norris.

Andy had lifted the ban on the wilderness area, since the biker problem seemed to be over. Hank, the wrangler who led the ride, agreed with me that it was a good place to head, since the long, steep trail would aid in building up Belle's windpower.

When we reached the top of the ridge, we paused for the horses to rest and the people to take pictures. I studied the work the Forest Service had done and admired the way they'd repaired the damage.

Finally we made our way down to the meadow. We were ambling along through the wildflowers when we heard the distant roar of machines.

Hank and I looked at each other. Not the bikers again!

"All right, everyone, let's get out of here," Hank announced. "Head back up the trail right now."

I knew he was particularly worried about a couple of the guests, the Brennans, who had just moved up into the advanced group. They were both quick learners, but they didn't have a lot of experience yet and might not be able to handle horses spooked by the noisy trail bikes.

"Move along," Hank urged, riding up alongside the Brennans. The group turned and began to jog back the way we'd come.

The noisy roar grew louder, and four bikes came into view. The front rider looked familiar and I squinted, trying to get a better look at him.

He spotted Belle and me at the same time, pointed his bike right at us, and gunned the motor.

I paused for a second, trying to make out his face. Yes, it was Dennis Dunleavy, a boy in Drew's class who was always getting into trouble.

Prize-Winning Horse, Maybe

I turned Belle and we started after the others but the bike kept coming at us. I heard the scream of the engine grow louder and louder. We broke into a gallop.

The bike roared. Dennis yelled insults over the noise.

Belle was in a flat-out run now, terrified by the monster chasing her.

Suddenly a rabbit darted across our path. Belle leaped to the side, then reared.

I left the saddle and hit the ground hard.

I caught a glimpse of Belle's eyes, huge with panic. Her front legs pawed the air. Came down. Missed me by inches.

Then she was off, running for her life.

chapter 6

"Belle!" I tried to scream. I couldn't make a sound. The breath had been knocked out of my chest.

The biker circled around me. Dennis's fat face peered down at me. Then he glanced over his shoulder and took off.

I heard hoofbeats replace the fading roar of the bike-monsters.

Hank leaned over me. "Chris, are you okay?"

I nodded and tried to say, "Go get Belle." Still no sound came out. I pointed in Belle's direction, jabbing the air frantically.

More hoofbeats. Mrs. Morris knelt beside me. Dad's Mrs. Morris. "Chris, I'm not sure if you remember, but I'm a nurse. Does anything hurt? Can you move your legs and arms?"

I nodded and tried to push out the word. Belle.

"She's winded," Mrs. Morris told Hank. "Why don't you go after her horse and I'll check her over."

"You sure?" Hank's faded-blue eyes were anxious.

"Uh-uh-elle!" I managed to grunt out.

"Okay, Chris, I'll get her. Don't you worry," Hank promised.

I lay back, finally able to relax a little. Mrs. Morris went over my legs, my arms, my neck as she asked if this, this or this hurt. No, no, no, I shook my head. I had to admit, she was real gentle and in a way, it was kind of nice to be fussed over.

The other riders showed up, asking about me. Mrs. Morris told them I seemed okay, but asked them not to hover too close.

In a minute or two I was able to take in a full breath and get the words out. "Did he catch her? Can you see?" I tried to sit up.

"Lie still, Chris," Mrs. Morris said. "Yes, Hank has her. She looks fine. They're on their way back now. Now, tell me if this hurts." She pressed along my back.

"It's just a bit sore, that's all. Is Belle limping? Can you see the reins? Did she get tangled in the reins?"

"Hank has the reins, and Belle isn't limping as far as I can tell."

"Can I sit up now? Please?" I begged.

Mrs. Morris laughed. "Boy, they sure raise tough kids on these ranches, don't they? Okay, slowly now." She helped me up.

Hank was leading Belle at a walk, to cool her down from her run. She didn't seem to be limping, but wasn't she favoring her right foreleg just the tiniest bit?

"Are you all right, Chris?" Mr. Singer asked. He and the others had dismounted and I realized they had been talking among themselves for the last little while.

"I'm fine." I tried to smile, to prove it.

"Did you get a good look at him, Chris?" Mr. Singer asked. "Can you identify the biker?"

"Yes, I know him. It was Dennis Dunleavy, a boy in Drew's class at school."

"That's great!" Mr. Singer pounded his fist into his hand. "She nailed him! He'll get what's coming to him!"

There were other comments like, "Throw the book at the punk!" and "Lock 'em all away." "For life," someone added.

I was watching Belle. She was still breathing hard, but was beginning to settle down. I squinted, peering at her. Yes, I was sure she was stepping a little too lightly on her right foreleg.

By the time they reached us, I was on my feet. I threw my arms around Belle's neck and buried my face in her mane. She nickered softly, as if apologizing for dumping me out of the saddle.

Then I knelt down and ran my hands over her legs. The right knee was swollen. Not much, but definitely swollen. I looked up at Hank.

"It's not bad, Chris," he told me. "Just that one

59

knee is a mite sore. Cold compresses and a good rest should fix it up in no time."

"What about the race?" I asked.

He shrugged. "We'll just have to wait and see. She might be fine by then, she might not."

"She's not running if she's not one hundred percent okay."

"Of course not," Hank agreed. "But it's just a slight swelling. It could have been a lot worse."

That started Mr. Singer off again, and the other guests joined in the chorus. There was talk of arrest warrants and so on, but I left it all up to them. I hated Dennis for terrifying my horse, but I was a lot more concerned about her than I was about him.

We made our way back to the ranch, with me leading Belle at a slow walk.

Hank and I stayed in the barn working on Belle while the others went in to phone the Forest Service. I wanted to call the vet—and hang the cost!— but Hank finally convinced me it wasn't needed. Wranglers were used to treating this kind of injury all the time. It was really minor, although it was major to Belle and me.

Maggie, Drew and the others came back from their trail ride and heard the whole story. Everyone agreed that the one bright spot was the bikers were now identified. After they all left, I stayed behind with Belle.

"Chris? Where are you?" Mrs. Morris called a little while later from the barn door.

"Back here in Belle's stall." By then I'd put a cold

compress on Belle's knee, spread extra layers of fresh bedding on the floor and was grooming her from stem to stern, discussing the entire matter with her in a soft voice to let her know the nightmare was over.

Mrs. Morris leaned on the half-door with one of the other guests behind her. "Doctor Ruiz thinks your horse is getting better treatment than you are."

I glanced at him in surprise. "But you deliver babies, Doctor Ruiz."

He chuckled. "That's my specialty, but I can also give a battered cowgirl a checkup. When your father returns from the range, I think he'd be relieved to know you don't have any serious injuries."

"Uh, okay, but make it quick. It's almost time to change Belle's compress again." I continued working on a snarl in her mane.

"You mean . . . here?" Doctor Ruiz said. "Don't you think you ought to come down to the house where I can look at you properly?"

"This isn't the first time I've parted company with a saddle, Doctor. I just had the wind knocked out of me, that's all. If I get a bit stiff, Dad can rub some liniment on me later." I showed him the can we use for the horses.

Mrs. Morris grinned, Doctor Ruiz shook his head, but I stuck by my guns. He did a once-over, found nothing beyond a few bruises, like I said he would, and left. I put a fresh cold compress on Belle's knee.

* * *

By Sunday night, when Mom made her regular phone call, the swelling had gone down in Belle's knee. I began to wonder if it might be strong enough for the race, a week off, but I wasn't holding onto hope.

"Hi, honey," Mom said. "How's life in the mountains these days?"

"Not as quiet as usual." I knew one reason Mom hated ranch life so much was that nothing much ever happened. She loved the bright lights, crowds and excitement of the cities.

"Why? What's up? Did Drew's new puppy decide to play tag with a skunk again?"

That was the only real news I'd had to give her the last time we talked.

"No, he's been real good recently, for a puppy. But do you remember those bikers I told you about before?" I went on to tell her the whole story.

"Chris, are you sure you're not hurt?" Mom asked. "You're not hiding anything from your poor old mother, are you?"

"No, honest. Doctor Ruiz checked me every day until he and his family left. I'm fine, and Belle's getting better." Then I had to tell her all about our race plans.

"If Belle's up to running, I'm sure you'll win, honey." She always believed I could do anything, and be the best at everything.

"How about your career? Have you heard from that friend's cousin who works in Branson with all the country western stars?"

"No, but Jim calls me every night, and he says his cousin is working on it—could be any day now." Her voice went a little soft when she mentioned his name.

"He calls *every* night?" Mom moved around a lot, singing at a lounge for a gig or two, then traveling on to different clubs, sometimes hitting three or four cities in a single week. Even me, her daughter, couldn't keep up with her all the time.

"Or I call him, once I know where I'm staying." Her voice was still soft. "He's a real nice man, Chris. A real gentleman."

"Mom, what are you trying to say? Are you *dating* him?"

She laughed, that deep, throaty Glorinda Lee chuckle, Glorinda Lee being her stage name. In real life, she's Linda Lee Hopkins Bradley. At least, it used to be Bradley.

"Now, Chris, honey, how can I be dating a man who stays put in Phoenix when I'm zipping all over the country? We're friends, that's all."

I was quiet a moment, trying to count the weeks since she first mentioned meeting this guy, Jim. "You've been friends for a while now, haven't you?"

"Well . . . yes." She sounded pleased. "Long-distance friends, of course," she added.

First Dad and Mrs. Morris, now this. I wished I could stop the world from spinning. Keep life from changing.

"Um, Mom . . . there's a lady staying here for a month, Mrs. Morris. Her husband died a couple of

63

years ago, but they used to come to the ranch together every summer. I don't know if you remember her. Amanda Morris? She's a nurse."

"Chris, honey, except for you, I can't remember a thing about my years on the ranch. All I recall is horses, cows, trees, mountains, and feeling bored, bored, bored. You were the only bright spot in the whole world back then. Why are you asking me about one of the guests?"

"Well, um . . . Dad . . . uh . . ." I couldn't go on.

She didn't say anything for a moment. "Are you trying to tell me your father is dating this lady?"

"Not exactly. He says they're just friends . . . maybe like you and Jim . . . ?"

"I see. How do *you* feel about it, Chris?"

I sighed. "I don't *know* how I feel about it, I'm kinda . . . mixed up."

"That's only natural," Mom said. "Tell me what you think. Do you like this Amanda Morris?"

So I explained how deep-down nice she was, and how I wished she wasn't, and about Dad being happy, and how I felt unhappy about not being happy for him.

"Don't be so hard on yourself, Chris," she said. "You have good reason to feel the way you do. But I know your dad pretty well—" again that throaty chuckle "—and he's not a man to rush into anything. She's only a visitor and once she goes home, who knows what will happen? I'm willing to bet you'll have plenty of time to get used to whatever comes down the road."

"You think so?" I felt my shoulders relax a little. "That would make it easier, I guess."

"Trust me, honey, your father is the most laid-back cowboy I've ever met, and that's saying something. He thinks long and hard before he makes up his mind about anything important. It took him a full year to decide to ask me out on our first date."

"No kidding," I said. "I didn't know that."

"Oh yes, I thought he'd never get round to it." She went on to tell me more about their courting days. As always, I felt sad that he couldn't live his life away from the ranch, and she couldn't live her life on it, but I'd long ago accepted that as plain fact and there was no fixing it.

I felt better after talking to Mom. I went out into the starry night and walked over to the barn to check on Belle. The swelling was so faint you almost couldn't feel it, and she wasn't limping a bit, but I decided another cold compress wouldn't hurt. While I worked on her, I explained the situation with Dad, and she listened carefully.

I finished by saying, "So I guess we'll just wait and see what comes next, Belle. Just like you and the race. Maybe you'll be ready, maybe you won't. I'll do all I can to help you, but if it isn't meant to be, I won't cry over it."

But I crossed my fingers when I said it. I surely did want to win that race. Real bad.

chapter 7

Starting the next day, Dad and I agreed it was okay to begin exercising Belle, taking it real easy at first. Slowly I worked her up, keeping a keen eye on her knee, which now showed no sign of swelling. But I always stopped at the teensiest hint that she was favoring that leg.

By Thursday, we were up to a slow lope. Even if the knee stayed fine, I wondered if she'd be ready to race on Sunday, without a chance for plenty of hard runs to prepare her. Dad, Maggie, Hank, and I went back and forth discussing the situation, but couldn't come to any firm conclusion.

"Telephone, Chris!" Drew called as he ran down from the main house at noon. I was using my lunch hour to work Belle in the lower pasture by the pond.

"Who is it?" I asked.

"Officer Adams, from the Forest Service," Drew said.

"Okay, keep Belle going for me, will you?" I brought her to a halt beside him. "She's warmed up now and I don't want her to stand around waiting."

"Sure. Slow lope, right?" He hopped on as soon as I slid off.

"Yup. No faster. And keep a close watch on her knee. Thanks, Drew." I ran for the house, wondering what Officer Adams wanted.

"Miss Bradley?" the ranger said. "We've decided to press charges against the biker who harassed you and your horse. We're charging his three friends too. Would you be free to come down to Town Hall tomorrow morning and testify for the Federal Magistrate at the hearing? We need to hear your side of the story. We also want you to make a positive identification of Dunleavy."

"Identify Dennis?" I'd been hoping I'd never have to see him again. "Well, I guess so, if you're sure you need me."

"I'm afraid we do. I hope it won't be a problem. We'd also like the group who was with you that day to appear, or at least some of them. Would the wrangler, Hank, be around right now?"

"He's in the dining room. I'll go get him." I ran to fetch him, then told Dad and Andy what was up. When Hank was finished, Andy spoke to Officer Adams to firm up the plan.

The next morning, a whole bunch of us piled into

the Double Diamond van. Some of the guests who were on the ride that day had already gone home, but Mrs. Morris, Mr. Singer and a couple of others were still at the ranch and were glad to come with us. Naturally, Hank, Dad, Andy and Drew came along too.

I wasn't nervous until we walked into the courtroom. It wasn't a fancy place like you see in the movies, just a plain room with a table on a platform for the judge—or what they called the Federal Magistrate. But with the flags and the official seals of Colorado and the United States hanging up there, it was kind of awesome.

Then I spotted Dennis. He sat with three of his friends—who had to be the other bikers—on a bench along the wall. They slumped back, real casual-like, but they didn't fool me. They were all scared, except for Dennis. He looked just as mean and ornery as ever. He was a big, pudding-soft boy with thick lips and piggy little eyes.

Somehow I ended up sitting between Dad and Mrs. Morris near the back, with the rest of our gang spread out around us. Officer Adams caught my eye and gave a thumbs-up sign, which helped me relax a bit.

It wasn't long before I was way beyond relaxed— I was bored, bored, bored. There was a lot of lawyer-talk and almost-whispered conversations with the judge.

Finally some people I didn't know were called to the witness chair, but it wasn't anything like the movies. Instead of the lawyers booming out questions and making speeches to the "Ladies and Gentlemen of the Jury," you could hardly hear a word said. There was no jury, for one thing, and no one thought it important for anyone but the judge to know what was going on.

I was almost dozing off when I heard my name called. I was so startled I jumped right up and shouted "Present!" just like I was in school.

A few people smiled. Dennis Dunleavy snickered.

He made me so mad! I stalked up to the witness chair and plunked myself down, scowling at him.

They handed me the Bible and I raised my right hand, swearing to "tell the whole truth and nothing but the truth" in a loud voice. At least I had the decency to let the folks in the back of the room know what was going on.

"Please state your name," the man said.

I did.

The judge took over then. "Miss Bradley, please tell us in your own words what happened a week ago yesterday."

"Dennis Dunleavy scared my horse, Belle, half to death," I said, still speaking up for the people in the back. "He drove his bike right at us, on purpose. He's never been anything but trouble anyway. Back in second grade, he stole my friend Drew's lunch—"

"Ah, let's stick to recent events," the judge said. "Tell us exactly what happened from the time you arrived at the wilderness area."

Louise Ladd

So I did, making sure every ear in that courtroom heard my opinion of people who tear up wildflowers and attack innocent horses. I finished by saying, "Now, I don't know exactly what you have in mind, Judge, but I have an idea of the best way to teach Dennis and his mean-minded friends a lesson they won't soon forget."

The judge blinked. He'd been staring at me while I told my story, his mouth open a little, so I guess I'd impressed him. "I'd be . . . interested in your idea, Miss Bradley."

"Well," I began, wiggling around in the chair to make myself more comfortable, "Dennis Dunleavy is one of the laziest kids you'd ever hope to not meet. If he saw a dime on the sidewalk, he'd tell someone else to pick it up and hand it over to him. Besides that, he's fat, so—"

"Hey, wait a minute!" Dennis shouted, standing up. "She can't call me—"

"Sit down!" the judge ordered.

"But—" Dennis began.

"Sit down! And be quiet!" The judge glared at him.

Dennis sat. And shut his mouth.

"Go on, Miss Bradley," the judge said.

"Well, as I was saying, he's fat and lazy," I cheerfully repeated. "And what does a fat, lazy person hate more than anything? Hard work, that's what. It seems to me, since he and his friends tore up the wilderness area, they ought to spend a good bit of time fixing up the damage. The Forest Service re-

70

paired it once, then that bunch came back and dug more ruts. Besides that, I'll bet there are a few more spots in the National Forest that could use the work of four boys who have nothing better to do with their time. Am I right, Officer Adams?"

The ranger grinned. "Quite a few more areas need attention, judge. Digging fence holes, planting trees, shoring up slopes likely to erode, cleaning up litter . . . I imagine we could keep four boys pretty busy for a while."

I glanced over at the bench. Dennis and his buddies were exchanging looks of pure horror.

The judge noticed too. He smiled at me. "We have a few more witnesses to hear from before I pass judgment, but I'll keep your advice in mind, Miss Bradley."

"Thank you, sir. Can I go now? I've said my piece."

"Yes, you may return to your seat."

I'm not real sure about this, but I think he gave me a wink as I stood up.

After that, Hank, Mrs. Morris, Mr. Singer and the others told their side of the story. I noticed they followed my example and spoke right up for all to hear.

The only surprise came when Mrs. Morris told the judge how scared she felt when she saw me hit the ground. Her voice wavered a little for a moment, but she quickly got back into her nurse-treating-the-maybe-injured-patient style of talking.

Finally all the stories were finished and the

judge leaned back in his chair. He closed his eyes for a moment, then spoke directly to Dennis and his buddies.

"One of you, Mr. Dunleavy, harassed Miss Bradley and her horse, but all four of you have admitted you were illegally riding motor bikes in a Designated Wilderness Area, on at least two occasions. That is against the law, and you know it. In addition, as I see it, you are all accomplices to the harassment charges. Therefore, I sentence each of you to perform one hundred hours of work for the National Forest Service."

"One hundred hours . . ." Dennis choked out.

"At forty hours a week," the judge said, "that comes to a mere two and a half weeks. By that time, school will be starting. However, if Officer Adams reports he is having the slightest bit of trouble with any of you, I will immediately double the sentence to two hundred hours. That will keep you busy after school and on weekends for quite some time."

He banged his gavel on the table and it was all over. Four boys left that courtroom looking mighty unhappy.

Hank drove our Double Diamond group to the best Mexican restaurant in town and we had ourselves a real good lunch.

Time speeded up and suddenly it was Sunday morning. Was Belle ready to race that afternoon? We had to make the decision.

Prize-Winning Horse, Maybe

I desperately wanted the answer to be yes. Not only because I needed the five-hundred-dollar prize, but because I wanted the whole town to see how fast—and how beautiful—my mare was.

But I was the one who kept saying no. Dad, Hank, Maggie, and I—with Drew listening in—batted it back and forth over pancakes, bacon and scrambled eggs. They kept pointing out that the swelling and the limp had been gone for a week and that a horse in such good condition didn't need to run flat-out every day of training. They said Belle was looking in top form and would be eager to race. They all said yes, yes, yes, let her try it.

But I wasn't convinced. I worried she might be hurt somehow. Maybe her knee would swell up again and cause a permanent injury. Maybe pushing her to win would be asking too much after the time she'd spent taking it easy. No prize money, no glory of winning, was enough to make up for causing my mare any type of damage.

The plates were scraped clean and the coffee pot was empty and still we hadn't come to a decision.

Drew hadn't said a word. As I mentioned, he was allowed to listen in, but his advice wasn't asked for.

As we stood up to leave, he announced, "I have an idea."

"What is it?" I asked.

"You've forgotten to ask the expert," he said.

We all began to talk at once, insulted. If Dad, Maggie, Hank and I weren't experts on horses, who was?

Louise Ladd

"Doctor Cooper, the vet, of course," Drew said. "You told me she would be going to the fair. Why don't we take Belle down this afternoon and she could take a look at her. If she says yes, then Belle will be there, ready to run. If she says no, it only means that your mare will be taking an extra ride in the horse trailer, which she doesn't mind anyway."

"Why didn't I think of that?" I said.

"Because your brain is so full of your horse, you don't have room for brilliant ideas," he said.

I punched him on the shoulder, just hard enough. He grinned and strolled away, whistling off-key.

Dad drove the pickup pulling the horse trailer, with Drew and me squeezed into the front seat. Somehow we made room for Serena when we picked her up at the Lazy B. We got to the fair grounds in the early afternoon. The race wasn't scheduled until five o'clock so we had plenty of time to find Doctor Cooper. Before we left home, I'd called her office, just to check, and the answering service lady told me she was already at the fair.

Dad parked the horse van under a shade tree in a field near the fair grounds and I made sure Belle had water and a little hay to nibble on if she got bored. Then we went off to find Doctor Cooper.

An empty patch of pasture just outside of town had been turned into Fantasy Land. Music came from a dozen different places, competing with the noise of the crowd. A Ferris Wheel soared up into

74

the sky, the merry-go-round whirled, bumper cars crashed and banged with happy shouts from the drivers, the spinning-dish ride set off shrieks of laughter from dizzy kids.

Red and white tents were scattered everywhere, pennants flying from their peaks. You could play games, buy hot dogs or cotton candy, and admire the things people grew, everything from giant tomatoes, to jars of jam, to ears of corn. The baking-contest tent smelled like pure heaven, with rows and rows of tables piled with homemade pies, cakes, breads, and cookies.

"How are we going to find Doctor Cooper in this crowd?" I asked.

"If you were a veterinarian, where would you head?" Dad teased.

"The livestock section, of course!" I sniffed the air. "It must be in that direction," I said, pointing upwind. There's no mistaking the barnyard scent of animals.

We found Doctor Cooper and her family admiring one of the largest hogs I'd ever seen. He was washed to pink perfection and even his hooves were shined spotless.

I went up to her and explained the decision we had to make soon.

"Sure, no problem." Doctor Cooper said. She was a tall lady, with an easy smile. Her husband said he'd take care of their three-year-old son. A minute later, we were on our way over to Belle.

I backed her out of the trailer. She gazed around

75

at all the sights, alert and interested, not at all nervous.

"Walk her around for me, Chris," Doctor Cooper suggested after feeling her legs carefully. I led Belle down the field and back again. Doctor Cooper watched closely. "Now jog her."

I didn't want to saddle her until I was sure she was going to race, so I trotted beside her, holding the lead rope to her halter.

"I'd like to see her move with you on board," Doctor Cooper said.

I threw the bridle on Belle, then Dad gave me a leg up and, bareback, we loped around in a wide circle.

We came to a halt in front of Doctor Cooper and, holding my breath, I waited for the verdict.

"She looks magnificent," the vet said. "And ready to race."

"You're *sure*?" I asked.

"As sure as I can be," she said. "I'll be watching, rooting for the both of you."

"Wa-hooooo! Allll riiight!" I threw my hat in the air, my hopes suddenly spinning as high as the top of the Ferris Wheel.

chapter 8

"Belle, you're going to run your first race," I said. "Now, don't be nervous, because we all know you'll win."

She turned her head and peered at me, wondering what I was doing with her hind foot. Before we left the ranch, I'd groomed her until her chestnut coat glowed, but after seeing that big hog's shiny hooves, I decided to finish the job right down to her toes. I'd sent Serena and Drew off to borrow a dab of whatever the hog's owner used and now I was polishing away.

"Chris, you're missing all the fun of the fair," Serena said, coming around the corner of the trailer. She was holding something behind her back.

"Can't leave Belle," I grunted.

"I'll horse-sit if you want," she offered. "You should at least try the cotton candy."

"It's almost time for the race." I gave the last hoof a final rub.

"I knew you'd say that. Here."

I looked up. She was holding out a big cone of pink spun sugar. I grinned. "Thanks."

While I ate, enjoying the way the fluffy stuff melted in my mouth, the gang from the Double Diamond began to wander over. Hank had arrived soon after we did, with a vanload of guests and all the staff that could be spared.

One by one, Maggie, Jamie, Andy, the Singers, Mrs. Morris, and all the rest came up to wish us luck. Then Dad said the words that made my stomach jump.

"Are you ready, Chris?" He gave me a hug. "It's race time."

The whole group of us, with Belle in the center, made our way through the crowds to the top of the racetrack. It wasn't a fancy course, just a quarter-mile stretch marked off with plastic ribbons tied to stakes in the ground. Without bleachers, people had dragged over boxes and barrels, whatever they could find to stand on to see over the heads in front.

The other horses and their riders were grouped at the top of the track, except for Mr. Jenkins and his Skittles. They stayed at a distance, the stallion prancing around, switching his tail and shaking his head.

"Chuck shouldn't have entered him," Andy Diamond said, frowning. "If he goes off the course, someone in the crowd will get hurt."

"I talked to Chuck earlier," Dad said. "If the race committee sees any sign of a problem, Skittles will be disqualified immediately. Chuck thinks he can keep him quiet. He's been training him with other horses, teaching him racetrack behavior. I guess we'll have to see if the lessons took."

Everyone wished us luck again. Then I led Belle over to the group of riders and their horses, saying hi to Ms. Cummings and Mr. Harmon and a couple of others who greeted me.

"Where's the starting gate?" I asked Mr. Harmon. In all the books and movies about racing, there was a fancy contraption with stalls that the horses lined up in.

"There isn't one," he said. "This is just a simple church fair. See that white chalk mark? That's the starting line. We stay behind it and wait for the gun to go off."

"Riders, please mount up," a tinny voice announced over a loudspeaker.

I could feel my heart banging against my ribs when I hopped up on Belle. She stood quiet, gazing around with curiosity at the crowd and the other horses.

"Riders, take your place at the gate, or in other words, the chalk mark," the tinny voice ordered.

I'd been given a cloth gizmo with two big number 4's painted on it. It went over my head and tied at the waist so the numbers hung on my chest and back. That meant I took the fourth lane, between the old Appaloosa, Jackie, on our right and Mr. Harmon's Pilgrim on the left. Athena, the fast buckskin owned by Wally Winthrop, and one of the main horses to beat, was in the number 7 spot.

When we were all lined up, Chuck Jenkins brought Skittles into the number 1 lane. Or tried to. The stallion danced around, crossing the chalk mark twice. The second time Mr. Jenkins backed him up, the tin voice blared, "Control that horse or he's out."

Mr. Jenkins tried—and he's a darn fine rider too—but the noise and the crowd were too much. Skittles swiveled his hindquarters sideways and crossed the line again.

"That's it, Jenkins. You're disqualified. Please remove your horse."

Mr. Jenkins' mouth made a thin line of disappointment, but he didn't say a word, just turned the bay around and rode off.

That was a break for us. Now Belle and I faced only two horses who were serious competition. Pilgrim, right next to us, and Athena, ridden by Wally, who "had more money than horse sense," according to the lady who ran the Gold Mine Stables.

Now if only Belle didn't bolt the gate before the signal!

"Riders, are you ready?" the tinny voice asked.

We all nodded.

"At the sound of the gun . . ." the voice warned.

I stopped feeling nervous and scared and excited

and focused only on Belle, telling her with my hands, legs, seat, and voice to get ready, but wait. She did what I asked.

"Five, four, three, two, one, BANG!"

We leaped forward in an instant, Belle's powerful stride taking us right out front. Her neck stretched out and I felt her legs pounding the ground, pushing her faster and faster.

Pilgrim was a split second behind us, but in moments he caught up. Belle saw him and poured on more speed. She was top mare—no mere gelding was going to outrun her!

On our right, the other mare Athena was running neck and neck with us. I saw her eyeing us, not liking what she saw. The horses in between had dropped behind and I couldn't see them.

Pilgrim pulled up even again, and Belle ran harder, faster. Athena kept pace, Wally whipping her hard.

Halfway down the course.

Pilgrim had dropped back even with my shoulders.

Athena veered toward us. Wally tried to straighten her out, but she wasn't having it.

Athena angled toward Belle, teeth bared.

Belle ignored her, racing straight for the finish line, legs pounding, one long line of flowing speed.

Pilgrim pulled up even, dropped back.

The finish line was just ahead.

Athena was next to us, running head to head with Belle.

I felt the slightest thump.

Belle broke stride for a split second.

She recovered instantly, but Athena was in front by a nose.

The finish line flashed past.

We'd lost.

Belle and I took our time slowing down, then heading back up the track. For the first time, I noticed the crowd was roaring, a flood of noise like river rapids washing over us. I kept my eyes fixed on Belle, patting her neck, telling her, "It's okay, Belle, you did your best, your very, very best. You were beautiful. You were perfect . . ."

Dad and all the others were waiting for us. I slid off the saddle into his arms, not hearing a word anyone around me said.

After a moment, I pushed myself away and tried to give him a grin. Shrugging, I said, "Now I know what Doctor Cooper and Mr. Harmon meant when they said, 'That's what makes horse racing.' "

Dad, wordless, squeezed my shoulder.

"Excuse me, please, I've got to take Belle back to the trailer." I pushed through the crowd, leading my mare at a slow pace to cool her down. People tried to talk to me, but I just smiled and nodded and didn't answer.

I was walking Belle around and around the trailer, still cooling her off, when suddenly I came face to face with Amanda Morris.

I don't know how it happened. I was fine, then

suddenly I was in her arms, sobbing my fool head off.

She held me for a long, long time. The tears kept coming like the spring rains you think will never stop. She was soft and warm and gentle and said little murmuring things that don't mean much and mean everything.

Finally, finally, I slowed down. My chest stopped heaving so hard and the tears dried to a trickle. I pulled back a bit and she handed me a fistful of tissues. Just as I began to dab at my eyes, I got the hiccups.

I was so surprised I giggled to hide my embarrassment. "Wh—hic!—what the—hic!—oh, heck!—hic!"

She began to chuckle. The next thing I knew, I was laughing just as had as I'd been crying, and all the while trying to squeeze a sentence out. "Th—hic! Thank you—hic!—I don't—hic!—know what's wr-wrong—hic!—with me!"

Mrs. Morris was too busy laughing to answer. She pulled out more tissues and dabbed at her own eyes.

"Chris! Chris!" Serena and Drew ran up to us.

"There's been a protest!" Serena said.

"Mr. Harmon!" Drew added.

"He says he saw that other horse bump you," Serena said.

"The race committee is talking about it right now," Drew said. "Come on!"

"Wait a minute!" I said. "What are you saying?"

"If Athena bumped you, it's not a fair win," Drew said. "They could disqualify her and that means *you* won!"

"You're kidding!" I couldn't take it in.

"Did you feel it, Chris?" Mrs. Morris asked. "Did the other horse run into you?"

"Just for a second," I said. "But I didn't think it meant anything. Wally couldn't control her. She was running her own race."

"Let's go talk to the committee," Mrs. Morris said.

"I'd better bring Belle. She's still not completely cooled down. She needs to keep walking."

Serena laughed. "You and your horse! She always comes first, doesn't she?"

"Of course," I said, surprised she'd even asked the question.

When we got to the tent booth where all the officials were gathered, everyone was shouting at once. As soon as they saw me, they all began to shout at *me*.

Dad took over and, in his easy way, soon had them all listening quietly while I explained what happened.

Finally, the head of the committee, a Mr. Sanchez, said, "We've had a number of witnesses confirm Mr. Harmon's story. Where is W.W. Winthrop, the owner of Athena?"

"Here I am." I'd noticed Wally hanging in the back of the crowd. Now he stepped forward.

Prize-Winning Horse, Maybe

"Did your horse bump Miss Bradley's horse?" Mr. Sanchez demanded.

"Sir, I honestly don't know." His face had turned peach-pink with embarrassment. "I haven't been riding long, and I was too busy to notice. I don't remember if she did or didn't."

"Since a number of people say she did, would you have any objection if we assume they are telling the truth?" Mr. Sanchez said.

"No, sir. I want to win the race fair and square. If I made a mistake, it wouldn't be right to take the prize money," Wally said.

A number of eyebrows went up in surprise at his honesty, and a few people even clapped. I have to admit, I was more than a little bit impressed.

"Good, son, good." Mr. Sanchez slapped Wally on the back. "You're a true sportsman."

Then he turned to his committee. "Are we agreed then?"

They nodded.

"Miss Bradley, you are now the official winner of the race!"

After that, there was an announcement over the loudspeakers, then the award ceremony, which I sort of floated through.

Mostly I remember the circle of flowers they draped around Belle's neck, and the way she stood so alert and quiet during all the fuss. I was bursting with pride, to think she was my own horse and everyone admired her so much.

85

When they handed me the check I'd dreamed of, I glanced at it, then gave it to Dad to put in his wallet for safekeeping. The money was sure welcome, but right then, other things were more important.

When almost everyone drifted away, I thanked Mr. Harmon for speaking up for me. Then I found Wally loading Athena into her trailer and thanked him.

"I'm just sorry it happened," he said. "I should never have entered the race in the first place. I don't have enough experience for something like this." He looked pretty darn miserable.

"Hey, experience takes time," I said. "You've got a real good mare, and if you keep working on her, she'll turn into a well-mannered horse."

"That's just what I plan to do," he said quietly, then turned away.

"And you earned yourself a lot of respect from all those folks by being so honest," I pointed out. "You should go home feeling good."

He looked back at me with a small smile, which almost made him look happy. "Thanks. I'll try to do that."

I noticed that after I left, a few of the race committee members went up to him and by the time he drove off, he was relaxed and smiling a whole lot more.

Dad was waiting for me with Serena, Drew, and Mrs. Morris. "Are you finally ready to enjoy the rest of the fair, Chris?" he asked.

I studied the bright tents and spinning rides and listened to the happy, excited screams and shouts. "I don't know, Dad. I was thinking it might be nice to go somewhere quiet, like that little restaurant that's on the way home. Just the five of us."

"The five—" Dad broke off and glanced at Mrs. Morris. Serena, Drew, himself and me made four. Mrs. Morris made five.

"After all, it's a special occasion," I pointed out. "We have a lot to celebrate, don't we?"

"Yes," Dad said. "We sure do." He put one arm around me and one around Amanda Morris. "Then what are we waiting for? Let's go!"

We had a real nice time that night.